PRECIOUS - THE NITWIT

PRECIOUS - THE NITWIT

George Ohler

iUniverse, Inc.
New York   Bloomington

PRECIOUS - THE NITWIT

iUniverse books may be ordered through booksellers or by contacting:

*iUniverse
1663 Liberty Drive
Bloomington, IN 47403
www.iuniverse.com
1-800-Authors (1-800-288-4677)*

*Because of the dynamic nature of the Internet, any Web addresses or
links contained in this book may have changed since publication and may
no longer be valid.*

*ISBN: 978-1-4401-4379-3 (pbk)
ISBN: 978-1-4401-4380-9 (ebk)*

Library of Congress Control Number: 2009928279

Printed in the United States of America

iUniverse rev. date: 5/12/2009

Contents

Chapter I

Me and You and a Dog Named Who?

Jim Johnson looked suspiciously at his wife, Mary. "What are you doing?"

"I'm just reading the Sunday paper."

It was Sunday morning and the couple were sitting in the breakfast room of their large two story home in the suburbs. The room has a bay window which overlooked their large backyard which sloped past the back picket fence down to the bayou. The backyard was immaculate with large trees on the side, flower beds in the middle and stone step paths to wander among the flora.

Jim was proud of his yard. He had planted every tree and every flower himself. He had even put in all the beds and put out the lawn himself. He was especially proud of a little area behind the garage that looked out over the bayou. He had put in a small patio with a fountain surrounded by gardenias. Overlooking the patio and bayou, as well, was a swing in which Jim had intertwined lights. This was a special place he had created for Mary.

Jim greatly enjoyed looking out of the bay window on Sunday mornings. However, this Sunday morning he was not looking out the window; he was studying his wife because he knew she was hatching a plot.

"You're looking at the classifieds. You're looking in the "Pets for Sale" Section."

"Oh, am I. I didn't even notice I was in that section."

"Mary, look, we agreed that we would wait. We decided that we should wait a while before owning another dog."

Mary looked at her husband intently, "How long is 'a while'?"

Jim picked up a section of the Sunday paper and pretended to read it rather than look directly at Mary, "I don't know. Maybe six months. At the longest, maybe a year."

"Six months! A year! I don't want to wait that long without a dog."

Jim put the paper down and turned back to his wife, "Honey, we decided we would wait some time before we have another dog. Besides, we won't ever have another dog as well trained as 'Fluffy' was."

"You're right, she was perfect."

"So, we will wait."

"Yes, but the next dog could be just as perfect."

Jim turned to Mary. He was getting ready to raise his voice, but upon looking into her beautiful brown eyes, he determined to calm down. He loved her dearly, and thought she was the most beautiful girl he had ever seen. They had met in college. He was tall, relatively handsome and dated a number of pretty women, but had never considered a serious relationship. He met Mary through a church club when they were seniors in college. She was a strikingly beautiful mix of Italian and Native American with high cheekbones and long dark hair. She also was extremely nice to everyone. All of Jim's family and friends agreed she was probably the nicest lady they had ever met. And Jim realized that they were correct. It was one of the rare cases of true love at first sight for both Jim and Mary. He asked her to marry him just a few weeks after they started dating and she, of course, said yes immediately.

They both had worked hard. He worked during the day in a lumber yard and went to night school at the university for his graduate degrees. Mary taught math in high school and also worked in retail during the summer vacations.

Their hard work had paid off. Jim landed a job at a prestigious accounting firm and they were able to build their dream home. They bought Fluffy immediately after settling in. They had an extremely happy marriage. However, as with most couples, they would often have "discussions" such as this one.

"Mary, you agreed!"

"Yes,"

"So, we agree, we will wait."

"Yes, I guess, at least for a little bit."

The next evening, Jim pulled into the driveway after work. He was very tired. He hated Mondays. For that matter, he was not very thrilled with Tuesdays through Fridays, either. He was an accountant, and fairly successful. However, his office job was just too routine. He knew he should not complain. He was good in accounting, and at least his job did not entail the difficulties of many other occupations. Still, he could not wait to get home in the evenings to spend time with his wife and their dog.

Jim walked into the kitchen from the garage, poured himself a glass of orange juice and sat down. The house was quiet. He did not like it. He missed their dog. He enjoyed letting Fluffy out in the evening and playing with her. She was fun and loving. Always gentle around any person or animal she met while with her owners. She was a good guard dog ,even though she seldom barked and had never really attacked anything. However, if she felt there was danger, as when a stranger would be in the driveway or backyard, then she would bark furiously to attempt to scare the stranger away and warn her owners of this unknown person. It saddened Jim that Fluffy, even though she lived a long time for a dog, could not have lived even longer.

Yes, Jim definitely missed the enjoyment of being greeted by their pet in the evening. Maybe they should think about having another dog, especially since Mary wanted another one so much.

Just then Mary pulled into the garage. Jim prepared himself to cheer her up as she entered the house.

"Hi, dear," Mary said brightly, kissing him on the cheek. "How was your day? My day was pretty good. I'm going to put supper on. I am cooking your favorite."

Jim could not believe how perky Mary was. He stammered "My day was okay. What did you do at work today?"

"Not much. However during my lunch hour I went on the internet and guess what? There are three breeders in the general area who raise corgis, the type of dog we're looking for. One is near my work. She has a female who had puppies a couple of weeks ago. The dogs will be wormed, have shots and be registered. And they should be ready in just three to four weeks. Isn't that wonderful?"

"Oh, no."

"No, really, we'll just look at them. She'll call me when she is ready to show the puppies and I can run by during my lunch hour to look at them. OK?"

"Well, OK."

"Wonderful."

Three weeks later Mary called Jim at his work. "The puppies are ready for me to see. I am going at lunch to see them and we can discuss which one we want at dinner."

"Wait. I thought you were just going to look. Aren't we jumping the gun here? We aren't even sure we want to get a dog."

"Oh, I will just look. We can discuss it at dinner."

That evening when John arrived home Mary was already home. She was looking at the computer.

"Look, Jim, the breeder sent over digital pictures of the two puppies that are for sale. Come look. This is the one I like." Mary said pointing to a cute puppy.

Jim looked at the picture of the first puppy then looked at the other puppy. He stared transfixed. It looked like a tiny fox puppy, only cuter. It was the cutest, sweetest looking puppy he had ever seen.

"I think this one on the left is much cuter, Mary."

"You do?"

"Yes, look at how cute it is. Look at that face."

"Yes, now that you mention it, she is cuter, and I have to admit she is even cuter in person. The only reason I thought of the other one, is that the cuter one is smaller. The breeder said that she is small for a Welsh corgi."

"I know, but it is definitely much cuter. It looks like she would have a very friendly personality."

"Does this mean that we can get her?"

"Well, I didn't say that."

"Please Jim. You know I will take good care of her. She will be even better than Fluffy. Just look at that face! How can you resist?"

"Well, alright."

"Oh thank you! I love you!" Mary said throwing her arms around Jim.

"Well, when should we pick her up?"

"I just have to call the breeder and set up a time. She wants cash. I can pick up the puppy probably next week after work and bring her right home."

"What day next week?"

"What about Monday?"

"That would be good. Are you sure you don't want me to be there?"

"No, the breeder will provide a carrying crate, all the papers, everything. You just go to work Monday and by the time you get home I will be here with our new puppy. I even know what I want to call her."

"What do you want to call her?"

"Precious."

"Yes, from looking at the picture, the name fits."

The next morning Mary called Jim at work. "It's all set! I pick up Precious Monday evening after work. Barbara, the breeder, is giving Precious her shots and will have her ready.

Jim had to admit to himself that he was excited. He also could not wait to have Precious. "That's great."

Chapter II

Precious Moments

The remainder of the week seemed to drag on by for Mary and Jim. Jim rushed home Monday evening. As he pulled into the garage, he noticed some weeds sticking out of the flower beds. He should have gone in to change his suit first, but being compulsive; Jim walked back out to the front yard and bent over to pull the few weeds.

Just then his wife pulled into the driveway and on into the garage.

Jim wanted to go run to see Precious, but there were just a few weeds left to finish.

Mary stepped out onto the front porch. In her arms was Precious.

She was even cuter than in her picture. She looked like a baby fox only even cuter!

"My gosh! She's even cuter than the picture!"

"Isn't she? She is so soft and cuddly. Here Jim, you take her."

Jim reached out carefully. It was like cuddling a small fur ball. Precious sniffed him then gingerly licked his face.

"I bought everything she needs," Mary said. "Precious has a nice comfy bed, dog food, a new combination food/ water bowl, squeaky toys, chew toys, and plush toys."

"You go on in and set her up. I will be right in."

As soon as Jim came in, he sat on the floor and called the puppy. Precious ran to him.

They snuggled. They hugged. Precious then lay flat on her back as a sign for Jim to stroke her belly.

As Jim stroked the puppy's belly gently, Precious emitted an almost purring sound, very soothing. Precious was very relaxed. Jim was very relaxed and enjoying the puppy.

All of a sudden, quick as lighting, Precious bit Jim on the hand.

"OW!" Jim exclaimed.

"Jim, what happened?"

"Precious bit me."

"Oh, she is just probably teething."

"No, this was a bite."

"Oh, I am sure she was just cutting teeth. Or maybe you hit a sore spot. Be careful with her."

Jim reached for Precious very carefully; Precious lay on her back and emitted her purring sound. Jim petted her and stroked her. Again, even before he could see it coming, Precious bit him, hard.

"OW! She did it again."

"You're just not doing it right. You need to be more patient."

"I am patient! I don't understand. I think something's a bit off. I think she might be schizophrenic – a nitwit!"

"Nonsense, let's eat dinner. Set up the table, I have Precious' food ready. Come here, Precious."

Precious came, looked at the food and ran back to attack her pile of toys.

"Huh," Mary said. "She should be hungry. I don't know why she is not eating. We can leave the food out and she can eat when she is ready."

Jim and Mary decided to eat dinner in the breakfast room rather than the formal dining room. The breakfast room opened up to the family room where they had put all of Precious' toys and where she enjoyed playing.

When they finished dinner, Mary started putting the dishes in the dishwasher. "I think I'll take Precious out to the backyard," Jim said. "Maybe it will help her run off some of her energy. Hopefully, she won't dig in the yard too much."

As soon as they were in the backyard, Precious began to dig in the flower beds.

"No, Precious, don't! Bad dog!"

Just then Mary came out "What's wrong, Jim? Is something the matter with Precious?"

"No. She is just being her usual self, she's just being a nitwit.

Jim went back to play with Precious. This time everything went well until Jim went to get up and as he turned around, Precious bit him on the back of the leg. Not a nip, but a bite which drew blood.

"Ow! Now she drew blood."

"Oh, dear, don't be such a baby," Mary said as they went back into the house. " Maybe she is just hungry. Here Precious. Come eat something."

Precious just stared at them.

"Let's take her back out to the backyard," Mary suggested. "That way she can roam around and get used to the outside."

Precious ran out the door almost before Jim could get it open. She ran to the first flower bed and started digging.

"Our petunias!" yelled Jim.

"Oh, they will be okay. She is just exploring."

After Jim shooed her from the third bed, within a few seconds, Precious started pulling the grass out of the lawn with her teeth.

The entire time Jim and Mary were trying to discourage her. Finally, Mary agreed it was time they brought Precious back inside. "She will get sick if she keeps eating all that mulch and grass."

Mary reached down to pull Precious from the grass and pick her up. As Mary tugged her gently, Precious turned and bit her on the hand.

"Ow!" Mary howled.

"See! It told you she will snap. You have to be careful."

"Oh, she's just nervous around her new surroundings. She's just tired. We can go in and put her to bed. She's just playful."

"She's a nitwit!" exclaimed Jim

"Yes, but a cute nitwit."

"She is very cute. And she is playful. She does have a lot of energy."

"Yes, I think she will be fine." Mary said. "Come, Precious, let's go in."

As Precious followed Mary in, she snapped at the back of Mary's legs.

"Ow! Ow! Ow! No Precious! Don't do that! That's not nice!"

After many attempts to coax Precious into her bed in the utility room, the couple finally succeeded by offering her a potato chip. She immediately went into the room.

When Jim and Mary went up to bed, Jim advised Mary that they probably would not get much sleep as Precious would be barking and whining all night. On the contrary, all was still and Jim and Mary were able to obtain much needed rest.

The next day Jim and Mary stayed home from work to take care of Precious. They looked forward to playing with Precious most of the day.

When they walked out into the backyard, Precious was a blur of activity. She ran to the neatly planted flower beds. She dug up the beds, she ate the flowers, and she ate lawn grass.

"No Precious! Don't do that! It's not good for you!"

Precious would stop a second look up at them with a happy smile and immediately return to her destruction. When they tried to gently pull her away, she would start to growl. If they continued to pull, she would do one of two things – she would stop, run into their arms, lick them, snuggle and then bite them on their arms or she would roll over for them to pat her on her tummy. She would then go back to her destructive behavior or she

17

would nip them sharply first and then return to her bad habits.

Mary did not understand. "Jim, why is she acting this way?"

"I don't know. Everything is new to her. She's probably just excited. We have to work with her, or she could have a screw loose. She could just be a nitwit."

"No. I think she just needs patience and guidance. And some training. We will work with her. I will buy some training books on puppies."

"Good. Hopefully, with effort and training tips, Precious will not only become the cutest dog anyone has ever seen, but also the best behaved."

Mary bought every training book on puppies she could find. She and Jim thoroughly read and then implemented every recommendation, suggestion and hint in the books. Northing worked other than bribery with food or a treat which would lead her, at least temporarily away from trouble or where they needed her to go, as when they needed to put her in her room. The edible enticements were much easier on Precious than "the leash".

Mary and Jim had bought several sizes and different types of halter leashes. They did not want to use a neck leash on Precious because of the strength she would use to resist might hurt her. So they tried the halter leash. Putting the halter on was like trying to put one on a small cougar. Mary and Jim ended up with many cuts, bites and bruises. And Precious was able to slip out of the halter no matter how hard they tried. So they finally had to resort to a collar leash. After super herculean efforts they were able to finally put the correct size collar on that stayed. They would then be able to attach the leash, again after extreme effort and fighting, to the collar. This was the extent of their success.

On all other activities, Precious would not obey. She was cute. She was playful. She would lick and snuggle. Then she would bite and scratch.

"She's a nitwit," exclaimed Jim.

"No, I think she is just frisky. She is just trying to become accustomed to everything. We just need to work with her and give her more time."

"Allright,"Jim agreed. "We will work with her and give her more time."

Chapter III

Saying "Hello" to the Neighbors

The following Sunday Jim and Mary decided to take Precious for a walk down the block and perhaps meet some of the neighbors. They had just walked a couple of houses when they met Mrs. Wilson and her granddaughter, Margaret.

Mrs. Wilson, who was a widow, was one of their oldest neighbors. She was the self-appointed "lookout" for the neighborhood. Jim and Mary said that there were three ways to send any message in the neighborhood – Telegram, Telephone, or Tell a Mrs. Wilson. Although a bit of a busybody, she was a very good neighbor, participating in charity drives, recycling efforts, and bringing homemade goodies to the neighbors.

The apple of her eye was Margaret, her granddaughter, an eight year old who helped her grandmother with all her charities and projects. She was a girl scout, straight A student and was always courteous to her peers as well as the adults in the neighborhood. She also loved animals.

Margaret's face lit up with a beaming smile as soon as she saw Precious.

"Oh my gosh! What a cute puppy! What kind of a dog is it?"

"It's a corgi," Mary said proudly. "She's a female."

"Can I pet her?" Margaret asked as she crouched down and extended her hand towards Precious.

"I don't think.." Jim started to say.

"Of course you can, Margaret," Mary interrupted.

Unfortunately, by this time, Precious had retreated behind Mary's leg.

"Come on, Precious, " Margaret coaxed. "I just want to pet you." She extended her hand out towards where Precious was hiding behind Mary's leg.

All of a sudden, Precious darted out, quickly licked Margaret's hand and then dashed back behind Mary's leg.

"Thank you for the puppy kiss, Precious," Margaret said, sitting down. "But I would like to pet you. Come here, girl."

Precious stood steadfastly behind Mary's leg.

"Come on, girl. Come here. I just want to be friends."

Precious pressed even harder against Mary's leg, apparently trying to become invisible.

After a few more minutes of trying to coax Precious out, Margaret got up with a sigh, "I guess she's just shy."

"Well, I must say her behavior is a little odd," declared Mrs. Wilson.

"I guess she is just a little frightened," Mary stated somewhat apologetically.

"At least she didn't bite Margaret like she does to us," mumbled Jim.

"I'm sorry. What did you say, Jim?" Mrs. Wilson asked starring intently, first at Jim and then down at Precious who was barely peeking out.

"I said, sorry if she gave a fright to Margaret, sorry about the fuss." Jim yelled out.

"Well, you don't have to shout," Mrs. Wilson said. "I heard you the first time. Still, I'm surprised at your puppy's behavior. She's the first dog I've seen that didn't come running to Margaret."

"Well, she did lick Margaret's hand," Mary said, somewhat defensively.

"Yes, but still, she seems a little odd to me. Are you sure your dog is alright?"

"I think she is just a little timid right now," Jim said. "It's probably been a little stressful for her meeting strangers."

"Strangers, we're not strangers!" declared Mrs. Wilson

"I know. I just think we'd better get Precious back," Jim said, taking the leash from Mary and pulling Precious around. He then took Mary by the arm and guided her back towards their house.

"It was good to see you and Margaret, Mrs. Wilson," Mary said over her shoulder as Jim was guiding her and Precious away.

"Goodbye, Precious," Margaret called out. "It was good to meet you. I hope we can become better friends," she said, somewhat dejectedly.

As they hurried back to their house, Mary asked Jim "Why such a hurry?"

"I don't know," Jim said. "I was just a little bit worried about what Precious would do."

"Oh, I don't think we needed to worry. Margaret is such a sweet girl."

"I know Precious would probably never snap at a child. She did, at least, lick Margaret's hand. I just think Precious might not be playing with a full deck. I think she is just a nitwit. I think we should try to keep her away from the neighbors, at least for the time being."

"Nonsense. I'm sure Precious and the neighbors will get along famously. They just need to get to know one another," Mary said as they went into the house.

The next evening, Jim came home from work. He immediately went to let Precious out of her room. He noticed that the door to her room was open. He looked in. Precious was not there. This was the day, once a month, that the maid service cleaned their house. Jim was afraid they might have accidentally let the dog out of her room.

"Here, Precious. Come here girl. Where are you?" Jim searched frantically throughout the house. He checked under the furniture and the cabinets. He even checked under every bed. He could not find Precious.

He went out to the backyard, and there found Precious rolling in the grass. She was covered with dirt and mud. "There you are! Come here girl." Jim then noticed the hole dug under the back gate. Jim was afraid that Precious would duck under the hole. "Here, girl, come here." Precious just sat and smiled at him.

Jim knew that if he tried to grab her, she would just run, probably thinking it was a game of tag. He also knew that even if he caught Precious, she would bite him. Precious did not like to be picked up, unless, of course, it was her idea. Jim did not want to get blood on his suit. Instead, he circled back into the house and came back with a potato chip. Oftentimes, Precious would not come for ordinary dog treats, but Jim and Mary discovered that Precious had a soft spot for potato chips. And even then, depending on her mood, it was not certain she would come.

Luckily, as soon as she saw the potato chip, she came running and Jim was able to lure her into her room, toss the potato chip in her mouth and close the door.

It was then that he noticed the answering machine on the phone blinking. There were several messages, all from the neighbors. Jim listened to the messages and immediately began to dial.

"Hello, Joe? Yes, this is Jim. Yes, I received your message. I am so sorry that Precious ruined your flowers. She just accidentally escaped from the backyard. We certainly will reimburse you for any costs. Yes, we will be sure that she will not get out again."

"Hello, Mrs. Adams? Yes, this is Jim Johnson. I am so sorry Precious pushed over your trash can. Oh, it was full with garbage. Well, I don't how such a little puppy could push over anything that heavy. Are you sure it was Precious? Oh, you saw her duck back under our fence. Well, we are very sorry. Yes, we will be sure to contain her in the future. Thank you for your understanding. Goodbye."

Mary walked into the house. She could immediately tell Jim was upset. "What happened?"

"Precious dug out from the backyard."

"Did you find her? Is she alright?"

"Yes, but she practically destroyed the entire neighborhood."

"Oh, I think that you are exaggerating. I think that ...." Mary could see that this was not a good time to discuss this with Jim.

"So, what are we going to do, Jim?"

"Well, first I am going to change my clothes. Then I will fill in the hole where she dug out. Then I am going to go to the hardware store and buy whatever we need to be certain that she will not be able to dig under the fence."

Jim found the perfect item at the store. It was a roll of hardened plastic edging that could be sunk into the ground at the desired depth and then could be secured to the fence.

By the time Jim returned, it was becoming dark. Mary was sitting on the back porch with Precious in her arms.

"Oh, Jim, that looks perfect. You're tired; we can do this tomorrow.

"Oh, no we're not. I'm not going to give her a chance to get back out!"

"Well then, we can help."

"No, you can't. She will get in the way."

"Fine, we will just sit here and cheer you on."

"Okay, but do not let her out of your arms. Do not let go of her."

"I promise."

"Fine," Jim said as he lugged the heavy roll of plastic to the fence.

Throughout the entire process Jim muttered to himself, "Oh, Jim, I promise that, if we buy another dog, I will take care of everything. You won't need to do anything. All you will have to do is play with the dog." "Yeah, Right! Maybe with some other dog, but this dog is just a nitwit!"

Chapter IV

Visitors

Mary answered the phone.

"Hello? Yes, Sheila. How are you? Yes, we are fine."

"I hear you have a new puppy."

"Yes, she's a corgi. We named her Precious. She is a cute bundle of fur."

"Great! When do we get to meet her?"

"Well, I don't know. We haven't had her very long and she's still not too sure of her surroundings. We haven't been able to train her yet."

"Perfect, I can help. You know how well behaved my dog is. I taught her all her commands myself."

"Yes, I know your dog is very good, but….."

"Great! We can't wait to see your puppy. Would Saturday afternoon be okay?"

"Well, yes, I guess that would be fine."

"Perfect, Ron and I will be there sometime after 2:00 and we look forward to seeing – what's the puppy's name again?"

"Precious."

Sheila and Ron arrived promptly at 2:00 pm Saturday. After hugging Mary and Jim, she rushed excitedly into the family room.

"Where's Precious? Where is the darling puppy?"

"She's in her room," Jim said. "I'll let her out."

As soon as Jim opened the door, Precious zoomed by, past him, through the kitchen and into the family room.

"Oh, Mary, she's even cuter than her picture that you sent to me over the internet!" exclaimed Sheila as she sat down on the floor to greet Precious.

Precious screeched to a halt. She looked bewildered at the strange people in the room.

"Maybe the rest of us should sit down," suggested Mary. "That way Sheila and Precious can bond better."

"Come on Precious, come here. You sure are a cute puppy. Come here. I just want to say 'Hello'." Sheila reached her hand out.

Precious just stared at Sheila, then bounded towards the outstretched hand. Almost as Sheila touched her, Precious leapt back.

"There, there, little puppy. I won't hurt you."

Precious sat and grinned at Sheila as Jim's sister gently held her hand out.

Then Precious leaped again towards Sheila, but again leaped back just an instant before Sheila could touch her.

This continued for several more times. Sheila lowered her hand and patted on the floor. "Precious, come here."

Precious started trotting around Sheila. Sheila raised herself on her knees and also started moving around in a circle trying to follow Precious. This went on for a few minutes, until Sheila finally stopped. "I'm getting dizzy."

"Don't stop now, dear," Ron said trying to suppress a laugh. "I think you are wearing her down."

"Well, I know one of us is wearing down, but I'm not going to give up. I'm going to pet this dog if it takes all day!"

"And all night," Jim interjected. He was sorry the minute he said it, but he just couldn't resist kidding his sister.

Sheila glanced disapprovingly at Jim and then stared back at Precious.

"Look, puppy, I just want to be friends. I just want to pet you." Sheila extended her hand back out.

Precious leapt toward her hand and then leapt back again.

"Looks like we're starting all over again," chuckled Ron.

"No, I think she will come around…" Sheila started to say, but was rudely interrupted. While she was looking at Ron, she still had her hand extended toward Precious. While Sheila's back was turned, Precious leapt forward and quickly nipped Sheila's hand.

"Oh my! I am so sorry, Sheila," Mary exclaimed. "Precious, you are a bad puppy. You should not bite. I think that Precious is just thinking that you are playing tag with her, Sheila. I'm sorry she nipped you."

"Oh, it's okay," said Sheila. "See, it did not even break the skin," she said, holding her hand out to show everyone.

Just then Precious leapt at Sheila's outstretched hand, nipped it even harder, then jumped back.

"OW! This time she did draw blood!" Sheila exclaimed in amazement.

"Maybe we had better put Precious up," declared Mary.

"No, I'm not giving up. I think the puppy is just confused. Perhaps she is slightly dysfunctional."

"She's a dingbat!" declared Ron.

"She's a nitwit!" declared Jim.

"I think nitwit, I mean Precious is just overwhelmed," Mary stated. "She's probably tired. I think we need to just put her back in her room."

George Ohler

"Yes, let's do that," said Jim as he ran to the kitchen to get a potato chip. He wanted to lure Precious to her room as quickly as possible

"Here, Precious. Come on girl," yelled Jim waving the potato chip.

"OUCH! She bit me again."

"I told you she was a dingbat," declared Ron.

"No, she's just a nitwit," yelled out Jim as he frantically waved the potato chip in from of Precious trying to get her attention.

Luckily, Precious trotted toward Jim. He then threw the potato chip into the puppy's room. Precious followed the treat and Jim shut the door behind her.

"I'm so sorry, Sheila," Mary apologized. "I think Precious just was too excited. Maybe we can go eat something."

"No, I think we need to go home now," Sheila said somewhat dejectedly. "We'll give Precious a chance to become more familiar with her surroundings and then we can come back. I'm not giving up on Precious. She's awfully cute. She is precious."

"She's a dingbat," added Ron.

"No, she's a nitwit,' added Jim. "Anyway, thank you for coming by. We love you and will talk to you later.

Jim turned to Mary, "You know, Precious really is a nitwit."

"Yes dear, but she is awfully cute and she is all ours."

"Yes, all ours."

Mary's mom, Lena Lowry, was the next person to see Precious. She came by Sunday. Lena was a first generation Italian immigrant. Jim always liked Mary's Mom as she was very hospitable, and man, could she cook! She was also very good with animals. She had been raised on a small farm and took care of all the usual farm animals. After they moved to the city, Mary's folks raised goats, chickens, rabbits, cats and dogs.

Mrs. Lowry, thus, loved animals, but at the same time she was "old school" and did not accept any disobedience from her family or from any of her animals.

Jim and Mary tried to dissuade Mrs. Lowry from seeing Precious.

"Nonsense, I want to see your new puppy. I'm sure we will get along famously."

Jim looked at Mary, who nodded her approval. She did not want to disagree with her Mom.

"Okay, Jim said as he hesitantly opened the door to Precious' room. "Here's Precious!" "The nitwit" he thought to himself.

Precious came out looked into the family room, then trotted right back into her room. "That was a quick greeting," stammered Jim.

"I guess she's just a little shy, Mom," Mary said.

"I think, for once, she is just using her head," thought Jim, but decided not to say it out loud.

"Well, no matter," declared Mrs. Lowry. "She and I can become acquainted at a later date. Meanwhile, you both come to my house and I will cook you some good spaghetti. You both look a little thin to me."

"Now, that's a plan!" Jim declared enthusiastically as he ushered the two ladies out the door.

Jim's dad, George, was the last member of the family to meet Precious in the initial few weeks of her becoming a member of the Johnson household.

George called Tuesday evening. Mary answered the phone. "Hello dad. How are you? Good. Is your hip still bothering you after your replacement surgery?"

"Well, not too much, Mary. If I turn too quickly, I occasionally might have a bit of pain. The reason I was calling is that my "better half" is visiting her sister, Jim's aunt, and I thought I might take the opportunity to fly down to see you and Jim."

"That would be great, Dad. Hold on, Jim is right here, I'll put him on."

"Hello dad. What's up?"

"I thought I might fly in to see you and Mary. I have reservations to fly in tomorrow. I'd like to see my favorite son."

"Dad, I'm your only son."

"I know, but you're still my favorite."

Jim chuckled. His dad always had a good sense of humor. "Terrific. I can try to get off early and meet you at the airport."

"No, I don't want you to have to take off early. I already have reservations at a hotel near the airport. I can only stay the one evening. Your mom and I have to go to the next door neighbor's anniversary party day after tomorrow. I did want to see you though. I will check into the hotel after I arrive. Then I will take a cab from there to your house. We can spend the evening together. And then you and Mary can drive me back to the hotel. We can have dinner there, my treat."

"Sounds terrific dad. And while you're here you can meet Precious."

"Oh, yeah, your sister told me about your new puppy."

"What did she say?"

"She said the puppy is very cute. A little fur ball. But that she is somewhat uncontrolled."

"Well, she is just a puppy. Mary and I have only just started to try to train her. She is a little frenetic, but I think with time she will calm down."

"I'm sure. Well, I look forward to seeing you."

Wednesday evening Jim and Mary both arrived home early. Soon after Jim's dad arrived.

After the initial hello's, Mary asked George "Well, are you ready to meet Precious?"

"Maybe we ought to wait a little while, hon. You know, until we can prepare Dad, I mean until Dad has a chance to settle in a little more."

"Nonsense, I'm fine. I'm anxious to meet the little fellow."

"She's a female dog, Dad."

"What's her name again?"

"Its nit..... I mean Precious. Mary named her."

"Well, I'm sure with a name like that, she must be adorable."

"I'll let her out, then," Mary said, hurrying to the kitchen.

"I probably need to warn you, Dad, that Precious is, well, a little dysfunctional. She might not take to you right away. She might seem somewhat anti-social. As I said, Mary and I have only had her a short while. We really haven't had much of a chance to train…"

Jim's words were cut off as a brown streak of fur flew by him towards his dad. George had just barely risen from the couch when Precious literally jumped and skyrocketed toward him.

"Oh my gosh!" declared Jim's dad as Precious hit him and pushed him back onto the couch. Precious alternately frantically licked and then nipped at George.

"Please, get her off!" George yelled.

Mary and Jim both rushed to the couch to try to pry Precious off of Jim's dad. Mary reached Precious first and tried to pull her away. Precious started growling. She seemed to become even more frantic. Mary kept pulling at Precious. "Jim, come help. I think Precious has a tooth caught in your dad's sweater."

Jim was torn between concern for his dad and trying to suppress hysterical laughter. He wished he had a video camera. He would probably win a prize in some video contest if he could film the tiny circus in front of him. Mary was pulling with all her might and Precious was getting more frantic by the second making it even harder for her to become disentangled.

Jim jumped in and was finally able to withdraw Precious' tooth as well as the entire puppy from off his dad.

"We better put Precious up now. I think she's getting a little tired," Jim yelled over his shoulder as he carried the wiggling, biting ball of fur back to her room. He somehow managed to open the door and tried to put

Precious down as gently as possible while quickly enough to shut the door before Precious could come back out.

"Man! Well, she's up. Who wants something to drink? Dad, how about you?"

"No, that all right, son. I'm fine. Perhaps we had better leave though. I'm getting a little hungry and it is a fairly long ride to the hotel."

"Oh, Dad, I'm so sorry about Precious," Mary declared. "She does seem to become just slightly frenetic sometimes."

"She's just a nitwit, Dad," Jim declared.

"Oh, no, I didn't mind. Really, George said. "She is very cute, at least from the little bit I was able to see of her. I can see why Mary named her Precious. She is awfully strong, though, for such a little puppy. Why don't we leave now so that we won't eat dinner too late?"

During dinner, both Jim and Mary apologized several times to George for their puppy's behavior.

"No, I really didn't mind," George said. "Precious is just a puppy and you both work. You haven't had much chance to train her yet. Because of your time constraints, perhaps you should consider someone else to train your puppy. You know, a professional."

"Well, I don't know, Mary said. "After all, Precious is still just a little puppy, and I think Jim and I can train her. I think she will calm down if we are just patient."

Jim didn't say anything in front of his dad. However, after they said goodbye to his dad, on the drive back, he brought up Precious's behavior.

"Maybe Dad is right, Mary. Maybe we do need to send her to an obedience school."

"I don't know, Jim. She's awfully small and she is still just a puppy."

"Yes, but perhaps it's better to train her right away. Right now she is just out of control and with her personality I don't know if we will be able to train her ourselves."

"I guess you are right. We will hire a dog trainer. I know that some of them will come to your house and train your dog at home. I've seen one advertised. She's a lady trainer. She has her business cards at our veterinarian's office. I will stop by tomorrow to pick up one of her cards and we can call her to come out and help."

Chapter V

Top Dog

Karen Albright was a very confident young woman. She was tall, nice looking, and athletic. She was outgoing, with an extroverted personality. She was very self-assured, especially in her career specialty, which was training dogs. She knew dogs. She understood dogs. And she knew she could befriend and train any dog. She started up her own dog training company wherein she would come to the dog owner's residence and train their dog along with the owners at their home. "Top Dog", her company, quickly became one of the most successful 'at owners' residence' dog training facilities in the city.

Karen rang the doorbell of Jim and Mary Johnson's residence. Karen noted that it was a large, nice looking house, very well tended. She thought that was a good sign. That they were also responsible pet owners and should respond well to her recommendations to attain and maintain a well behaved pet.

When she spoke to Mary Johnson, Karen stated that it would probably just take one week, every evening, to train Precious in the basics. Follow up visits might be necessary, but she did not think so.

Her first question to Mary on the phone had been, of course, "What kind of dog is Precious?"

"She is a Welsh corgi."

Karen was not as familiar with Welsh corgis as other breeds. Although, she had trained one at the start of her career, she tried to remember what the breed was like. She remembered it was slightly smaller than a medium size dog. It was approximately the size of a small beagle. Oh! She did remember. One of the first dogs she had trained was a corgi. It was probably the second most difficult dog she had ever trained. It was very difficult! Well, no matter, she now was more capable and experienced. She was sure she would not have any problems.

Mary Johnson answered the door. "Good evening. You must be Karen. Please come in. My husband, Jim and, of course, Precious, as well as I have been expecting you. We are looking forward to working with you. Jim is waiting in the family room and then when you are ready, we can let Precious out to begin.

"Good evening, Karen. Jim Johnson. Good to meet you. We appreciate your assistance in helping us train Precious. I am afraid she can be a handful."

"Oh, I don't think we will have any problems. I am used to working with all breeds, including the larger ones, which are considered harder to handle such as Dobermans and German Shepherds."

"Well, Precious is just a corgi. She is not a very big dog, but she is, might I say, a little frenetic."

"She's just enthusiastic," added Mary.

"I don't know, Mary. I think she is kind of wired. She is a bit of a nitwit."

"Nonsense," declared Mary.

"Well, let's get started," interjected Karen as they all sat down.

"Let me go over the program. First, I will become acquainted with the dog. On this initial visit I will bond with her and then do a few practice training exercises to ascertain what might be required. I will teach her to heal, sit, and walk along beside you first on a leash and then without one. She will learn to stay and only come when you call her."

"One of the problems we have now," Mary emphasized "is that she jumps up and down continually. She also runs around furiously, jumping on the furniture, and tearing around. Oh, and sometime she might bite."

"Yes, and she will bite, especially when you least expect it," interjected Jim.

"Oh, she just sort of nips."

"It draws blood."

"Well, why don't you let Precious in, and I can start."

Mary opened the utility door and let Precious in. Precious ran into the family room, looked up and saw Karen and stopped. Precious looked sideways at Karen and then smiled at her.

Karen exclaimed "Oh! What a cute little dog. No wonder you call her Precious. However, I did not realize how little she was. How old is she?"

" She is just a few weeks old "

"Well, she is little and young, but I guess it is good to start her training early. I should mention again, though, that I am accustomed to working with larger, slightly older dogs. But, no problem. Precious and I will get to know each other and we will work together side by side."

"Come, Precious. Come here."

Karen sat on the floor. "Come here, Precious. Come on over."

Precious grinned and ran into Karen's arms. "What a cute dog. Yes, you are. Yes, you are a good dog."

Precious rolled on her back and let Karen rub her tummy.

"Good dog. Oh, I think we are going to be doing fine."

And then Precious bit Karen on the arm.

"Bad dog! I am going to put this training collar on Precious and control her and run her through a series of drills.

"The first drill is to have the dog walk along with you. Come Precious." Precious followed Karen closely as she led Precious around the room.

"Now, Precious, stay." Karen held her hand over Precious and then dropped the leash. Precious stayed exactly as she was supposed to.

Karen continued with a series of five drills

"See, this is how you control your dog. We will do one more series of drills and then I think that will be enough for today."

When Karen pulled the leash, Precious just sat. Karen pulled on the leash, dragging Precious. Precious started to choke.

"Wait a minute!" exclaimed Mary. "You're hurting Precious."

"No, she is just trying to establish dominance. We are seeing who the top dog is. And it will just take a little more time and effort to train her.

Mary frowned, "I don't know."

"Trust me. In a week I will have Precious perfectly trained."

The remainder of the week was worse than the first training session.

Karen was at her wits end, and it seemed to Mary that Karen was too rough on Precious.

"I'm sorry Mr. Johnson, but I think we will have to just accept that Top Dog can't train Precious. You do not have to pay me anything else. Goodbye!"

After Karen left, Jim Turned to Mary "Well, what are we going to do? We can't continue to let her run rampant. She's just a nitwit."

"No she's not! I know, we will take her to a formal dog training school. There is one nearby. It's called "My Friend".

Chapter VI

Easy as 1, 2, 3

Since an individual trainer failed with Precious, Jim and Mary decided that, perhaps, a professional training school might work. So, the next day Jim called My Friend, the dog training school located close to their neighborhood.

"My Friend. This is Mack. How may I help you?"

"Yes, my name is Jim Johnson. My wife and I are interested in enrolling our dog in one of your training classes."

"Certainly, let me explain our training program to you."

"First don't you need to know about our dog? She is a little corgi pup…" Jim was not able to finish his sentence.

"First let me explain our program, and then I can obtain the details we require."

"Oh, okay, go on."

"Good. Well, basically, our training program is a three step program. First you leave your dog with us all day and night for two days. One of our handlers is assigned to train your dog, which is the second step. Then, the third day, you come back and the handler provides you with a behavior consultation for your dog. He then will work with you to instruct you on handling your dog. We call our program 1, 2, 3 because it is as easy as 1, 2, 3"

"Oh, I didn't realize that we would have to leave our dog overnight. I don't think my wife, Mary, would…."

Again, Jim was not able to finish his sentence before Mack interrupted.

"Sir, it is a requirement that you leave your dog here for the full two days. That gives our handler a chance to spend the time necessary to totally bond with and train your dog."

"Well, I guess we could leave her. I will have to discuss it with my wife. What does all this cost?"

"That depends on the type of dog. What breed is it? Pit Bull, German Shepherd, Doberman?"

"It's a Corgi."

"It's a what?"

"It's a Corgi. You know, small, furry, short legs, big ears. Looks somewhat like a small fox."

"Huh!"

" She is a Corgi. A Welsh corgi. Haven't you ever trained a corgi before?"

"Well, I am not sure. You say it's a small dog."

"Yes."

"How old is it – one year, two years, three years?"

"Well, it's just a puppy. It's only a few weeks old. It's Maybe seven or eight weeks old."

"Oh, we usually take dogs that are a little older and, also, we usually handle larger dogs. However, I'm sure we can work something out. When can you bring the dog by to leave off?"

"Well, as I said, I will have to speak to my wife. If she agrees, we could probably drop the dog off this coming Monday. I did have a question on the final day, when we are supposed to train with the dog. My wife and I both work, so should we take that whole day off from work?"

"No, I don't think that will be necessary. Can you, perhaps, take off work a little early and arrive here say by 4:00 p.m.?"

"I don't see why not. Let me just check with my wife and I will call you back."

"Roger," Mack said. "We will wait to hear from you."

As Jim hung up the phone, he wasn't too sure about this dog school. It sounded a little like a military or reform school for dogs. He wasn't sure that they would know how to handle a small puppy such as Precious. Nevertheless, he was certain that Precious did need some sort of training. At least they should try.

That is exactly what he told Mary in order to convince her. She finally agreed. Jim called the training school back and set up the appointment to leave off Precious on Monday evening.

Monday afternoon Jim and Mary loaded Precious into the car to take her to the dog training facility. Precious immediately knew that they were going somewhere she would not like. Mary had a harder time putting the leash on Precious than normal, even with Jim's assistance. By the time they were able to place the puppy in the car, Jim and Mary were exhausted. Then Precious became even more frantic. First she went over to sit in the driver's side so that Jim could not sit down to drive. Mary was finally able to drag Precious over to the passenger side, enduring numerous scratches and nips, just long enough for Jim to sit down to drive. Then the fun really began.

Precious wiggled and squirmed and nipped at Mary in order to escape. Luckily, Mary had her thickest gloves on so that she was able to hold onto the puppy despite the numerous bites.

Then the dog began to howl right into Jim's ear. It was similar to a coyote's yelp, only even higher pitched and almost deafening in the enclosed space. Luckily Jim was able to reach to the back floor for some tissue paper which he stuffed into his ear. He, of course, had previously moved the tissue box from the convenience of the front seat to the back floor. Jim knew that if he left the box in front, Precious would have torn the box and tissues to shreds in just a matter of minutes.

Though it seemed like one of the longest drives in their life, Jim, Mary and the howling puppy reached the training school fairly quickly.

The couple dragged Precious to the door and Mary pulled the puppy in, followed by Jim.

The inside of the building was pandemonium. There were at least a half dozen dogs barking and tugging on their leashes. All of the dogs were very large. One couple had two huge Dobermans. The man as well as the woman had both hands on the leash of their respective dog and were literally leaning backwards digging in their heels to avoid losing control of their dogs.

The Johnson's tiny puppy certainly stood out from the crowd. Jim was not certain what would happen with their little corgi. He was afraid she would either run or, perhaps, even be attacked by one of the large dogs. Instead, Precious trotted to the middle of the crowd. A couple of the largest dogs ventured over. Jim was ready to jump in front of the puppy and Mary in case the dogs attacked. Instead, the dogs just nuzzled Precious before their owner pulled them back. The remainder of the dogs stood staring at Precious or actually backed up as if in fear.

Jim told Mary to hang back while he went up to the counter to notify the receptionist of their arrival.

"Jim Johnson and that is my wife Mary with our dog Precious. We have an appointment to see Mack about enrolling Precious in your training school."

"Oh, yes, Mr. Johnson, Mack is our manager. He is expecting you. Please take a seat on that bench in the corner. Mack will be with you shortly."

Soon, all the other owners and their dogs disappeared into various parts of the building after their names were called.

Finally, a large, confident looking man strode towards them. From Mack's bearing, Jim thought to himself that Mack had probably been in the military or some type of law enforcement, probably working with guard dogs.

"Hi, I'm Mack," he announced as he shook Jim's hand vigorously.

"Yes, I'm Jim Johnson. This is my wife, Mary, and here is our dog, Precious."

Mack looked at Precious and his eyes widened. "Oh my, your dog is little. She is just a puppy!"

"Yes, that's what I told you, Mack."

"I know, but I really did not know that she would be quite so young and little."

"Yes, she's a puppy. But isn't it best to try to teach a dog as young as possible?"

"Well, I suppose so. It's just that we're used to working with larger, more mature dogs. However, I believe we can work with you. It just might be a little more difficult as we are not used to training such a little, young dog."

"But, you think you can train her?"

"Well, we can certainly do our best. As I have advised you, we will need to keep her here for a couple of days. We will assign one of our best handlers to her. He will work exclusively with her. By that, I mean only he will work with your dog. Then on the afternoon of the third day, the handler will consult with you on your dog's behavior. He will then work with you a little bit with your dog to reinforce the training she has received. Does that sound agreeable?"

"Yes, I guess so. What do you think Mary?"

"Well, I'm not sure. You know, Precious can be somewhat obstinate and even a little cranky. She might try to bite. You won't hurt her will you?"

"Mrs. Johnson, we here at My Friend are professionals. It is our business to train dogs, irrespective of their disposition. I'm sure you will be please with the results."

"Well, I guess that's okay then."

"Fine, let me get some papers for you to sign. We require ½ down now and the remainder when you pick up your dog. I will be right back."

"Do you think we are taking the correct course here, Jim?"

"Well, I think we must try this, Mary. Precious is somewhat out of control and this appears to be the best choice."

"All right, then. But will you be certain to check up on Precious tomorrow and the next day to be certain she is doing okay?"

"Yes, I promise. I will call both days to check on her."

"Good."

Mack returned with the paperwork. It consisted of a contract wherein the dog center agreed to do their best to train the dog. They would also provide a behavioral consultation and work the dog with the owner.

Jim and Mary read over the short contract and signed it. Jim paid Mack the required half payment.

"Good," Mack said. He stood up and shook Jim's hand. "Now, don't worry Mr. and Mrs. Johnson. We will take good care of Precious. I'm sure we will be able to instill a sense of obedience in Precious. We will see you Thursday afternoon."

Mary gave Mack a large bag of the dog's food as well as Precious' bed and a couple of the puppy's favorite chew toys.

As she handed the leash to Mack, Precious seemed to realize, finally, that she was going to be left in a strange place. She started to howl and pull on the leash. She pulled so hard, that Mack, not expecting such energy from such a small dog, almost fell over.

Mary rushed to the door. "Oh, I can't bear to look back. Precious is so upset. I just can't stand it."

"Don't worry, Mary. I'm sure everything will be fine," Jim hustled Mary out the front door. "I will call tomorrow to check on Precious' progress."

Jim called the following afternoon. The receptionist answered the phone.

"This is Jim Johnson. Is Mack there?"

"Oh, yes, Mr. Johnson. If you could please hold, I will transfer your call to Mack's office."

"This is Mack. How may I help you?"

"Mack, this is Jim Johnson. How did Precious' first day go?"

"Well, as we expected, she is quite a challenge. She is quite obstinate isn't she?"

"Yes, she is, but that is why we brought her to you. You will be able to train her, won't you?"

"Well, we are certainly doing our best."

"And you're not hurting her, are you? I know she can be cranky and somewhat aggressive sometimes. But she is just a small puppy after all."

"I promise we aren't hurting her, but you did bring up a good point, Mr. Johnson. She is so small and so young. You see, we are used to training larger, more mature dogs here."

"But you will be able to help won't you?"

"Well, we certainly are doing our best. You can call tomorrow and I will be able to give you a better progress report."

"Fine, I will call tomorrow at approximately the same time. Goodbye."

Wednesday afternoon Jim called the training center almost exactly the same time as the previous day.

"My Friend, this is the receptionist, how may I direct your call?"

"Yes, this is Jim Johnson. I would like to speak to Mack, please."

"Oh, Mr. Johnson, Mack is busy right now. He said if you called you could speak directly to your dog's handler. His name is Ian. I believe he is free now. If you would like, I can connect you to him."

"That would be fine."

"Please hold on and I will transfer you."

"Ian here, how may I help you?"

"Ian, this is Jim Johnson. I understand you are training our dog Precious.?"

"Oh, Precious. Yes, well, we are doing our best."

"What do you mean? You are training Precious, aren't you?"

"Well, it's just that she is so obstinate and cranky. And she seems to be all over the place. And yet she is so tiny and cute. We can't really use the methods that we normally are able to employ on the larger, more mature dogs. I just don't know what to do!"

"Ian, are you sobbing?"

"No, I'm fine, really fine, really, I'm fine. It's just that she is…"

" A nitwit?" Jim interposed.

"I was going to say that she is not "playing with a full deck", but now that you mentioned it, yes, she is a nitwit."

"Well, what should we do?"

"I guess we just stick to the schedule. I will work with precious again tomorrow. Then you and the missus come by tomorrow afternoon and meet with Mack.

Jim told Mary of his conversation with Ian.

"Mary, I don't think we should expect too much. I don't think the training center is having much success with training Precious."

"I'm afraid you're correct Jim. I hope they have been successful, but it does not sound like it."

Jim and Mary arrived at the training center the next afternoon. Jim walked up to the receptionist "Jim and Mary Johnson here to see Mack."

"Oh, yes, Mr. Johnson. Mack asked me to show you to his office as soon as you arrived. Please just follow me."

Jim and Mary did not have very long to wait before Mack arrived.

"Mr. and Mrs. Johnson, It is good to see you. Unfortunately, I am afraid we have not had much success in training Precious. She is obstinate and extremely headstrong. She is very hard to understand. She can be very loving one minute and then aggressive the next. She is slightly dysfunctional. We could normally deal with that behavior in larger, more mature dogs using stricter methods. However, as your dog is so small, well, she is still just a tiny puppy; there is not much we can do."

"So, what would you suggest, Mack," Jim asked. "I mean, we did pay you and we are supposed to receive a consultation."

"Well, I'm afraid this is the consultation, Mr. Johnson. We just were not successful with Precious. She flunked our training school. We will certainly be happy to refund your money as we are professionals and do not want to take your money if we have failed. Perhaps when Precious is older and hopefully larger, you can bring her back and we can try again, if you would like."

"No, you keep the money, Mack. We will just take Precious home. I guess it is up to Mary and I to now try to control Precious the best we can."

"Thank you Mr. Johnson, and good luck," You will need it" , thought Mack as Jim and Mary left with Precious.

Chapter VII

The Nitwit Disappears

Jim pulled into the garage after work. He was afraid that the cleaning person might still be at the house. Mary used the service every month to help her keep the house clean as she also worked full time. It was one of the few luxuries she afforded herself and Jim was hoping that it helped ease her workload a little bit. The primary problem in having the cleaning service come to the Johnson's house was, of course, the Johnson's dog.

Mary had given specific instructions to the cleaning service that there was a dog in the utility room and to not open the door so as to not let the dog out. And, prior to their getting Precious, it had worked very well, with neither the personnel nor the dog getting in each other's way.

Jim opened the door from the garage and looked over the backyard. He immediately noticed that the gate on the short picket fence which led to the bayou was open.

Jim rushed into the house to check on Precious. He looked into the utility room expecting Precious to come bounding out.

No Precious!

Jim looked through the entire house. No Precious!

Just then Mary came in. The expression on Jim's face immediately told her something was wrong. "Where's Precious?"

"I don't know. The gate in the back was open."

"We've got to find her."

"Don't worry, we'll find her. I'm going right now to look for her. I will ask all the neighbors if they've seen her."

Just then the phone rang.

Jim ran to answer the phone. "Maybe it's someone calling to say they've found Precious."

"We have your dog," the voiced on the phone declared.

"You do? Where did you find her? Who is this?"

"I'll do the talking. We want lots of money for your dog."

"Well sure, we can give you a reward."

"I'm not talking reward. I'm talking ransom."

"What do you mean?"

"We want $10,000. We will return your dog unharmed. But, we need the money by tomorrow."

"Wait, I can't have that much money ready in one day. Besides, how do I know you have the right dog. How do we know it's our dog?"

"Small, brown, fuzzy; very, very cute. Has a happy grin. Snuggles with you and then bites you viciously. Besides, we took her from your yard along the bayou"

Yes, that's the nitwit. I mean that's Precious. Look, just give me a little time and I will get the money. Just don't harm the nit, uh Precious."

"You have my word that we won't harm a hair on her head. We just want the money and then… OUCH!"

"What was that?"

"Your dog just bit me again."

"She does that. She doesn't mean to. I think she just has a quirk. She's just a nitwit. But she is our nitwit. Just don't hurt her. I just don't have the money in cash, but I will get as much as I can."

"No, we need $10,000. OUCH! OUCH! Well, look, maybe $10,000 is too much. Can you raise $5,000?"

"Maybe, but I don't know if I can obtain that much in one day. Can you give me a little more time, and I will try to come up with the money."

"No, one day is long enough. OUCH! Okay. Whatever you can raise in the one day, say $3500? OUCH!"

"I will try. I will withdraw all that I have in the savings, but I am not sure how much it will be."

"Okay. OUCH! Okay, just get as much cash as you can. I will call you tomorrow at 5:00 p.m. to arrange the swap. Just don't call the authorities."

"I promise. We won't. But can I have your word that you won't harm the Nitwit, I mean Precious. I know she is a handful and it's hard not to be mean to her."

"You have my word that I will not harm her. I might be a scoundrel and a dognapper, but I am a man of my word. Besides, she is very cute. Even if you want to punish her, she gives you that cute grin and then she can be very loving."

"I know. She's cute. She's loveable, but then she can snap. She just has a bit of a screw loose. She's just a nitwit."

"Yes, but you're right, she's a loveable nitwit. OUCH! I just want to return her to you and you can get me whatever you can have by tomorrow. I will call you back at 5:00 p.m."

Do we have a deal?"

"You have a deal"

As soon as Jim hung up the phone, Mary hugged him excitedly. "Someone found Precious? Are they sure it is Precious? Where is she? Are they going to bring her here or should we go get her? And it sounded like they wanted a reward. We can certainly give them a reward for finding Precious."

Jim started to tell Mary the true nature of the phone conversation. She was so happy and excited that he could not stand to tell her it was a "dognapping".

"Uh, yes, they found Precious. It's not one of the neighbors. I'm not sure who they are. But they will bring Precious home tomorrow."

"But we need to have her now. Did you tell them we can pick her up and give them the reward?"

"They will bring her tomorrow. It's a little late today."

"But…."

"Don't worry, dear, we'll have Precious tomorrow. I promise. Now let's eat a little something and go to bed early. We're both tired."

Jim and Mary were unable to sleep that night. Jim was worried as to what he was going to do tomorrow. Should he tell Mary the true situation? What if the man never called back? Should he call the police? He knew he was going to withdraw the money so he would have it just in case. But what would happen then?

Mary lay awake worrying about Precious. Yes, Precious was a little hard to handle. And she did have a mind of her own. She did seem to be a bit "addled". As Jim said often, maybe she did have a "screw loose". And, yes, as Jim often said, for which she always berated him, Precious might be a "nitwit". But she was such a loveable nitwit. And she was their nitwit.

She also wondered why the person who called to say they found Precious did not bring her right away, especially as they were going to give a reward. And she wondered about the phone conversation Jim and they had. It sounded funny. She was going to ask Jim exactly what the man said and exactly when tomorrow he was going to bring Precious home. Mary looked at the clock and it was 3:30 a.m.

Just then the doorbell rang.

Jim jumped out of bed, putting on his robe. "Who could that be at this time of night? I'll go down and check. You stay here."

"No, I'm going down with you."

Just in case, Jim grabbed a golf club from the closet.

They both crept down the stairs. As they approached the front door, they heard someone run from the door, jump in a car, and roar off.

Jim turned on the porch light and peered into the darkness watching the vehicle disappear down the street.

He looked down onto the porch. There lying in a large comfortable doggie bed was Precious.

"Mary! It's Precious!"

As soon as they got the door open, Precious woke up, jumped through the door and ran to greet both of them.

Mary grabbed Precious and hugged her eagerly. Mary handed Precious to Jim. "I have to get her some food and water. I bet she's hungry after her ordeal. She can sleep with us tonight. Poor little puppy! What have you been through?"

Precious seemed so happy to see Jim. She licked him, she smiled, and then she bit him. "OUCH! Why did you do that? What a nitwit!" Jim set Precious down. "Go see Mary."

As Precious ran off, Jim went out to the porch to pick up the doggie bed. Only then did he notice the note attached. He read the hastily scribbled lines.

"Here's your dog back. I promised I would return her unharmed, but forget any money. I just want to be done with her. She is the cutest dog I have ever seen. She is a small, brown ball of fluff. But she is also the most contrary, unpredictable animal I have ever seen. You were right. She's got a screw loose. She is just a nitwit."

Chapter VIII

Reunited and So Happy Again

The next Saturday Jim and Mary were in the backyard. They were trying to do some gardening, but, as usual, Precious was all over, interrupting any progress.

"Mary, come get Precious. She's digging in my new plant bed."

Mary ran to pick up Precious who was trying to run from her. They were going to play tag. Round and round the yard they ran until finally Precious stopped. She then ran and jumped up into Mary's arms, smiling and licking her. Then Precious was squirming to be let down.

"Jim, come hold Precious while I go get one of her toys to distract her."

As Jim held Precious in his arms, she smiled up at him. "Yes, you really are the cutest pup." Precious continued to smile up at Jim, licked him and then chomped down on his hand.

"OUCH!"

Mary turned, "What's wrong Jim?"

"Oh, nothing."

"Look how cute Precious is laying in your arms. Isn't it wonderful to have Precious home! " Mary exclaimed, disappearing into the house.

"Yes, wonderful to have her home", thought Jim as he worked to pull his hand from Precious' mouth. What a nitwit!